Edited by

Wade Hudson and Cheryl Willis Hudson

Foreword by Ashley Bryan

CROWN BOOKS FOR YOUNG READERS ♔ NEW YORK

Compilation copyright © 2018 by Just Us Books, Inc.

Cover art copyright © 2018 by Andrea Pippins

Decorations copyright © 2018 by James E. Ransome

Foreword copyright © 2018 by Ashley Bryan

Introduction copyright © 2018 by Wade Hudson and Cheryl Willis Hudson

"What Shall We Tell You?" copyright © 2018 by Wade Hudson, illustration copyright © 2018 by Floyd Cooper. "The Golden Rule" copyright © 2018 by Carole Boston Weatherford, illustration copyright © 2018 by Jeffery B. Weatherford. "A Thousand Winters" copyright © 2015 by Kwame Alexander, illustration copyright © 2018 by Ekua Holmes. "We, the People" copyright © 2018 by Rita Williams-Garcia. "Prayers of the Grandmothers" copyright © 2018 by Sharon M. Draper, illustration copyright © 2018 by Eric Velasquez. "You Are Here." copyright © 2018 by Denise Lewis Patrick, illustration copyright © 2018 by Nancy Devard. "Words Have Power" copyright © 2018 by Ellen Oh, photograph copyright © 2018 by Don Ha. "Kindness Is a Choice" copyright © 2018 by Jacqueline Woodson, illustration copyright © 2018 by Javaka Steptoe. "To Find a Friend" copyright © 2018 by Joseph Bruchac, photograph copyright © 2018 by Charles R. Smith Jr. "Get on Board" story-quilt copyright © 2018 by Cheryl Willis Hudson. "You Can Change the World" copyright © 2018 by Bernette G. Ford, illustration copyright © 2018 by George Ford. "Next" copyright © 2018 by Lesa Cline-Ransome, illustration copyright © 2018 by James E. Ransome. "Drumbeat for Change" copyright © 2018 by Kelly Starling Lyons, photograph copyright © 1966 by Bettmann Archive via Getty Images. "The Art of Mindfulness" copyright © 2018 by Evelyn Coleman, photograph copyright © 2018 by Zamani Feelings. "One Day Papí Drove Me to School" copyright © 2018 by Tony Medina, illustrations copyright © 2018 by Edel Rodriguez. "It Helps to Look at Old Front Page Headlines" copyright © 2018 by Marilyn Nelson, iPadology copyright © 2018 by Mansa K. Mussa. "All Nations Are Neighbors" and "I Wonder" copyright © 2018 by Margarita Engle, illustration copyright © 2018 by Rafael López. "When I Think of You" copyright © 2018 by Sharon G. Flake, photographs copyright © 2018 by Zamani Feelings. "a day of small things" copyright © 2018 by Tonya Bolden, illustration copyright © 2018 by Vanessa Brantley-Newton. "Dark-Brown Skin Is Beautiful" copyright © 2018 by Eleanora E. Tate, photograph copyright © 2018 by Chester Higgins Jr. "here is a poem of love and hope:" copyright © 2018 by the arnold adoff revocable living trust. Used by permission of the author. "We've Got You" poem and art copyright © 2018 by Pat Cummings. "How to Pass the Test" copyright © 2018 by Hena Khan, photographs copyright © 2018 by Stephan J. Hudson. "Where Are the Good People?" copyright © 2018 by Tameka Fryer Brown, illustration copyright © 2018 by Innosanto Nagara. "You Can Do It" copyright © 2018 by Jabari Asim, photo collage copyright © 2018 by Nina Crews. "Tell It in Your Own Way" essay and art copyright © 2018 by Roy Boney Jr. "What Songs Will Our Children Sing?" music and lyrics copyright © 2017 Curtis Hudson International Copyright Secured. All Rights Reserved. Transcribed and Engraved by David Isaac, photograph copyright © 2018 by Stephanie Berger. "You Too Can Fly" copyright © 2018 by Zetta Elliott, illustration copyright © 2018 by Laura Freeman. "Advice . . . (I'm Old-School Like That)" copyright © 2018 by Olugbemisola Rhuday-Perkovich. "A Talkin'-To" copyright © 2018 by Jason Reynolds, illustration copyright © 2018 by Andrea Pippins.

For photograph credits, please see page 87.

All rights reserved. Published in the United States by Crown Books for Young Readers, an imprint of Random House Children's Books, a division of Penguin Random House LLC, New York.

Crown and the colophon are registered trademarks of Penguin Random House LLC.

Visit us on the Web! rhcbooks.com

Educators and librarians, for a variety of teaching tools, visit us at RHTeachersLibrarians.com

Library of Congress Cataloging-in-Publication Data is available upon request.
ISBN 978-0-525-58042-3 (hardcover) | ISBN 978-0-525-58044-7 (ebook) | ISBN 978-0-525-58043-0 (lib. bdg.)

Art direction by Nicole de las Heras
Book design by Monique Razzouk and Carla Weise

MANUFACTURED IN CHINA
10 9 8 7 6 5 4 3 2 1
First Edition

Random House Children's Books supports the First Amendment and celebrates the right to read.

Dedicated to
those who advocate for and pursue a just society
and basic human rights for all people

Contents

Foreword

I'm sure just to touch this book, *We Rise, We Resist, We Raise Our Voices*, will lift your spirits. If you flip through all the creative gems put unto your hands and hearts by the gifts of people of color, we will hear your voices chanting praises.

Then, as you read, you will realize this is not a onetime read but a resource for rescue from any pitfalls of the day.

Stand up, reader, and cheer for the good fortune that offers you this book to live by.

Reading opens treasures, and this book is a treasure to enjoy.

"Having a safe space to imagine and dream and (re)invent yourself
is the first step to being happy and successful,
whatever road you choose to pursue."

—*Ashley Bryan*

Introduction

This book was inspired by our great-niece Jordyn. After the 2016 presidential election, she was distraught upon hearing who had won. She had heard the cruel and hateful words that had been spewed at women, those with disabilities, people of different faiths, and people of color. She had heard the talk aimed at "taking our country back." Though she was only seven, some of that language of hate stayed with her. When she found out who the new president would be, she was frightened and confused, worried that the world as she knew it was in imminent danger.

We were so troubled. We knew there were thousands—no, millions—of young people like Jordyn, and perhaps, like you, too, who were fearful about the future. What could we tell you? we wondered. What words of comfort could we offer? How could we reach out to you the way others had reached out to us when we were your age and faced difficult challenges that seemed too big for us to handle?

So the idea for this treasury was born. Yes, we are living in challenging times, but we created this book so you will know that you are part of a community that loves you and can give you tools to help navigate the present and the future.

We grew up in the segregated South, when life for us was much different than it is today. Racial discrimination, prejudice, and hatred against African Americans were pervasive. We were prohibited from attending school with White children, so we went to all-Black schools. We couldn't go to the public library that Whites used. We were forced to sit in a "special section" in movie theaters. We couldn't even try

on clothes or shoes from the stores downtown. Our parents had to purchase them, bring them home, and then see if they were a good fit. If they weren't, the items couldn't be returned. If there was no fountain designated "Colored" or "Negro" in the store, we had to wait until we got home to get a drink of water, or find another establishment that had a fountain for "us." Our parents were not allowed to vote.

This segregated but unequal system we were forced to endure was extremely trying and often frightening. Yet, in our all-Black communities, we were embraced by accepting arms, motivated by encouraging words, and sheltered by watchful eyes that probed for signs of lurking dangers seeking to engulf us. We were *loved!* We knew it! We could feel it!

Today's challenges are different from those of the 1950s and 1960s. But we have valuable advice to share with you, nuggets of sustenance for you just as there were for us when we were your age. We invited children's book creators with diverse voices to share their perspectives, words and images of encouragement, and hope and love for you. These talented and thoughtful authors and illustrators have already been creating wonderful books with you in mind.

Within this collection, there's a letter from a parent to her children on kindness; there's advice on how to become confident and mindful; there are words of wisdom about finding and keeping friends; there are reminders of how to use the Golden Rule, how to cope with bullying, and how to face internal uncertainty; and there's an essay on how young people can change the world.

Challenges, some seemingly daunting, will come and go. There will be dark days, and days with bright, warm sunshine. There will be periods of hope, and periods of despair. But when the dark days come, you must remember how the sun shone brightly on your face. When despair looms, you must grasp on to hope and lift it high for all to see. That way, you can face the challenges, no matter what they are, with the determination and confidence necessary not only to endure, but to grow in spite of them.

This book is for you! To inspire you, motivate you, offer you love and hope, and encourage you to help make a difference.

—*Wade Hudson and Cheryl Willis Hudson*

What Shall We Tell You?

Wade Hudson   Illustration by Floyd Cooper

What shall we tell you when our world sometimes seems dark and uninviting?

What shall we tell you when hateful words that wound and bully are thrown
   like bricks against a wall, shattering into debris?

What shall we tell you when respect for others and treating others as
   we wish to be treated appear as yesterday's borrowed wish?

What shall we tell you when our differences are juggled like fragile eggs
   that could be smashed at a moment's impulse?

What shall we tell you? What shall we tell you?

We shall tell you that love, like cream in milk, will rise to the top
   and hatred and distrust will be revealed as imposters.

We shall tell you that peace, desirable like a restful night
   after a long day at play, is not far away. Reach for it.

We shall tell you that respect for others, like a delicious ice cream bar
   dripping on holding fingers, tastes better than contempt.

We shall tell you that we love you, all of you! And because we love you,
   we will be there to help bring light to dark places.

We will be there with peace and justice as our weapons and love
   as a soothing salve to comfort and embrace.

We shall tell you that because we will be there for you,
   always be there for you, it will be all right! It will be all right!

The Golden Rule

Carole Boston Weatherford   Illustration by **Jeffery B. Weatherford**

Some form of the Golden Rule exists
in every major world religion.
In what may be the earliest version,
the ancient Egyptians commanded:
*Do for one who may do for you,
that you may cause him thus to do.*

Confucius first put the rule to paper:
*Do not do to others what you do not
    want them to do to you.*
By then the rule had been around
    for centuries.
One culture after another embraced
    the creed,
and one generation after another
    echoed it.

Jesus preached, *Do to others what you
    would have them do to you.*
Buddha instructed, *Hurt not others
    in ways that you yourself would
    find hurtful.*
Muhammad declared, *No one of you
    is a believer until he desires for his
    brother that which he desires for
    himself.*

This rule binds us as brothers
    and sisters.
The Tao teaches, *Regard your neighbor's
    gain as your own gain and your
    neighbor's loss as your own loss.*
The Sikhs simply say, *Treat others as you
    would be treated yourself.*

Zoroastrians proclaim, *That nature alone
    is good which refrains from doing unto
    another whatsoever is not good
    for itself.*
The Hindus deem this *the sum of duty.*
In Judaism, the Talmud concludes,
*This is the entire Law; all the rest is
    commentary.*

As Black Elk, the Ogala Lakota holy man,
    explains, *All things are our relatives;
    what we do to everything, we do to
    ourselves. All is really One.*
Many religions, many translations,
but one world, one yearning—
to love and be loved.

That is more precious than gold.

A Thousand Winters

Kwame Alexander   Illustration by **Ekua Holmes**

"The creative artist is the one wanting to make order out of chaos."   —Ursula Nordstrom

The other day
on the way
for bubble gum
ice cream (her favorite)
my six-year-old
cautions me
to slow down:

You are driving too fast,
    Dad, she exclaims,
with a worried frown
holding tears (she's not
    supposed to have yet.
    Or ever)
beneath her raised brow
And I don't want
the police
to take you
away
from me.

On another day,
we walk home
from school
like we have all year
waving at
the crossing guard
sloshing through
the puddled tunnel
passing the corner church
when she asks:
Am I going to vacation
    Bible school this year?

Yes
is what I would have said
without hesitation
before Charleston
but today,
my words are cold.
Hope is frozen.

Summer's here,
but it feels
like a thousand winters
and the world is not
such a beautiful place
anymore.
Dad, I asked you a
    question?
    she repeats.

Last night,
the sky was ablaze.
Bolts of lightning shot
across the night
like our very soul
was on fire
and I sat writing
next to a sea of flames
wondering . . .
if these are not times for
    poets
if words, sentences, and
    books aren't enough,
    anymore

if my first mistake was
    listening to NPR with her
    in the car
if this middle passage of
    murder is becoming
    normal
if those of us who jumped
    were the sane ones
if we can't survive this
    storm, how will our
    children?

How will our children?

She asks for two scoops
I give her one (it's before
    dinner)
plus a topping
the red, white, and blue
    sprinkles
disperse like little stars
across her face and shirt,
    and
she devours
her treat—cone and all—
    so fast
and so free
that when it disappears,
she's in disbelief.

So am I.

We, the People

Rita Williams-Garcia

My Dears,

It is my honor and privilege to reach out to you during this time of uncertainty and distress to offer a few words of encouragement. This should be a time of excitement about what our new leadership will bring, not only to our individual lives and to the nation, but to the world. However, because of what our leadership has shown us through words, gesture, and action, many of us have cause for concern. Cause for fear for ourselves, our family members, and our neighbors. Cause for anger. Cause for mistrust in not only our process but in what the new leadership will bring.

Know this: we as a people and as a nation have survived uncertainty, unjust and unequal treatment at the hands of the powerful. Our various histories and current-day struggles are stories of overcoming, with an eye on opportunity and freedom, even during the worst times.

In this nation we can lift our voices. To ensure that the Bill of Rights and Constitution are living documents, we must stand up and protect those documents through our words, voices, and art, and through our willingness to right wrongs in our own lives.

I encourage young people to be of service to yourselves by honoring your minds and bodies, and by taking steps to build upon your many dreams.

Be of service to your family. Take on one responsibility and be consistent with it.

Be of service to your community in small ways. Study together. Donate. Volunteer. Forget cliques. Build community. Invite others in.

Reject ignorance. Keep up with what is going on in government, whether it's local, national, or worldwide. If you can read, you can know! Even better, you can pose questions!

In a free society, that's what literate, concerned people do; they read, listen, and above all, ask questions.

Be of ultimate service to the nation by partaking in the process that those before you were barred from: Vote.

The nation's founders were not perfect, but they built a political system based on liberty, personal pursuits, and rights with laws to uphold them—particularly the right to disagree. They put in place the means to improve upon this system of government in anticipation of an evolving nation.

They did so, not knowing that the very system that they upheld in their times (slave-owning, oppression of women, etc.) would be in opposition to the more perfect union they sought to create. Nevertheless, in their wisdom, they incorporated checks and balances to protect the nation against the tyranny of the powerful, and to ensure a democratic union.

The founders didn't know that this would include all of us. And although they didn't have that complete and diverse vision of We, the People, they wrote and signed living documents that would protect and serve the rights, pursuits, and liberties of We, the People.

Yes. All of us. Not some of us. There's no backward time travel, but only the future. You must know and believe that you are the future and that you are charged with the challenge of making ourselves, our families, our communities a living and perfect union through your acts of service.

Write your letters. Ask the hard questions. Hold the leaders to their task, which is to serve and provide a future that ensures the rights, pursuits, and liberties of you. We, the People.

Prayers of the Grandmothers

Sharon M. Draper   Illustration by Eric Velasquez

I remember my grandma's home cookin',
She'd hum, and she'd mix, and she'd stir.
She could make buttered bones taste
  delicious,
If that's all the fixin's there were.
Stay safe, my child, she'd whisper.
Come home to me each night.
The sun is gold, the trees unfold
And danger hides from sight.

I remember my grandma's lap-naptimes,
Where dreams would lie wrapped in her
  arms.
She would sing of old pain and lost glory,
Of the long-ago days on the farms.
Don't talk back, she'd tell me.
Move not to left or right.
Stay safe, my child, she'd whisper.
Come home to me each night.

I remember my grandma's strong fingers,
As she brushed and she braided my hair.
My scalp and my brain would just tingle
As she wound her own memories there.
Let them see your hands, she said.
Don't run, just walk, hold tight.
Stay safe, my child, she'd whisper.
Come home to me each night.

I remember my grandma's old washtub.
It was battered and made out of tin.
Warm bubbles made baths seem like
  magic,
And nighttime and dreams could begin.
Breathe slowly, she would tell me.
Swallow pride and fright.
Stay safe, my child, she'd whisper.
Come home to me each night.

I remember my grandma's soft blankets
On a large, squeaky four-poster bed.
The faint smell of mothballs and cedar,
And her warm breathing close to my head.
The world is full of promise
And dreams you shall ignite.
So stay safe, my child, she'd whisper.
Come home to me each night.

I now give the grandmothers' warnings
With mac and cheese spoonfuls of love.
I show them the joy and the rainbows
Wrapped in hope on the wings of a dove.
Stay safe, my child, I whisper.
Come home to me each night.

You Are Here.

Denise Lewis Patrick   Illustration by **Nancy Devard**

Sometimes if you're traveling in a strange place and you get lost, you might look at a map and see the words: *You Are Here*. That map shows you where you are and where you've come from. It shows you a way to get where you want to be.

Many people have made this journey on Earth before you. We, who love you, have traveled through life, too. Our lives have created a map that you can always follow.

Long ago your people came across oceans of fear and cut through fields of wilderness to clear your path. We knew you would be coming.

Through our struggles we have made some bumpy roads smooth for you, because we have walked them over and over again, trying to find answers to hard questions. We have used our anger as a fire to light up the darkest moments. We have looked for and found friends to trust, and those friendships have made us all stronger. We have kept faith that when one way was blocked by giant stones, we would find other ways. And we have.

It's true that our roads sometimes got washed out by tears. So some of us learned to swim, some built bridges, and others kept their heads above the water until the water went down. And then we continued, because we knew you would be coming.

Now you are on your journey. You may meet people who don't understand you. People might say or do things that make you feel as if you don't belong. You may feel lost. You might even *be* lost. But stop a moment and remember that you have a map with you always.

You come from people who have never stopped finding a way, building roads, cutting paths—trying to give you many ways to get wherever you want to be. We knew you would be coming, and we are your life map in truth and spirit and memory. *You are here*, and we are here with you.

Words Have Power

Ellen Oh   Photograph by Don Ha

When I was a kid, I had a bullying problem. I was called terrible things. I was spit on. I was beat up. I was humiliated. All because I was a Korean American girl who didn't look anything like "White America." This was my introduction to racism.

"Why don't you go back to your own country?" strangers would shout at me.

They didn't understand that this is my country, the only country I've ever known. Where was I supposed to go? I wasn't a person to them, just a stereotype.

Encountering racism was painful, but it was nothing compared to witnessing what my parents had to deal with. At least I spoke perfect English. But my immigrant parents, with their broken English, have suffered far worse. As immigrants, they encountered humiliating racism and suffered crippling poverty, and yet they have never wavered in their love and support of their adopted country, their belief that the American dream had a place for them, too.

I was proud of them and ashamed of myself. I was the one who hid my lovingly packed kimbap lunch from my classmates to avoid being teased about eating "weird" food. I refused to speak Korean in public with my parents because I didn't want to stand out. I was embarrassed to be an Asian in a white country. But not my parents. Living in America didn't diminish their pride in their Korean culture and heritage. And when people sneered at their broken English, they reassured themselves that they spoke two other languages fluently—Korean and Japanese. When I think of all the humiliation they endured, I am both brokenhearted and proud.

Racism taught me to hate myself. But my parents taught me to be proud of my culture, my heritage—to be proud to be Korean even when faced with bigotry and hate, and despite my moments of self-loathing. At the worst of my bullying, my dad told me, "If someone hits you once, you hit them ten times harder." I learned the hard way that this was not the best advice. Especially for someone who was always angry. In fact, it was a recipe for disaster.

But it also taught me a valuable lesson. Anger is both a powerful tool and a dangerous weapon. It should be used wisely—channeled to give a person strength and conviction. You might start with anger, but you need to end up in another place. A better place. And the only way to do it is to engage others in dialogue.

Over the years, I have found that the best way to change someone else's mind is to sit down and talk and learn from one another. One should never underestimate the power of words. One should never underestimate the importance of changing one person's mind. Change happens one person at a time.

So now I must pass on that same pride my parents vested in me to my own children. I must remind them that hate comes from ignorance, and ignorance can only be countered by sharing ideas and experiences, the proof that we are all human.

Ellen Ha, age 9, and Janet Ha, age 1

Kindness Is a Choice

Jacqueline Woodson   Illustration by **Javaka Steptoe**

Dearest Toshi and Jackson Leroi,

Each morning before you leave for school, I say to you, Be safe. Be kind. I think some days that because you're both still young, you don't understand why I don't let you leave the house without looking into your eyes and saying these words.

I want you to see, through my own eyes, how much I mean what I say—that kindness is a choice. We can walk through the world choosing to think of others. Or we could not. Each morning when you walk out our door, I want you to ask yourselves—*What choice am I going to make today?* I want that choice to be Kindness. Because right now, all around you, the world is feeling unkind. As a child, I was taught that I am in the world but not of the world. This is what I want you to think when the world feels like it has lost its mind, when leaders don't feel like leaders, when adults lie and bully, when you know, in your brilliant and beautiful and loving hearts, the right thing to do and the right way to be.

Already I see it—in the letters home from teachers, *JL thinks of others when . . .* and *Toshi's kindness shines through.* So I know that some of what I'm saying is reaching you. Hold fast to it. Hold deep. Walk through each day and out of it, knowing the blanket of love each of you is wrapped in and ready to open that blanket to others.

I love you more than you know. And then some.
Mommy.

To Find a Friend

Joseph Bruchac   Photograph by Charles R. Smith Jr.

Look into the mirror.
What do you see there?
It seems to me that you might view
a friend there looking back at you.

If someone says that isn't true,
here's a few questions
I'd like to ask you.

Is a friend someone
who's always there?
Is a friend someone
who's going to share
everything good or bad?

A friend doesn't care
how tall you are.
It's not through height
that you see the North Star.

A friend doesn't care
what clothes you wear,
or about the color of your hair.
A friend sees how beautiful
   you are,
even on days when you're sad.

So look into that mirror
and when you smile
a smile will come
shining back at you.

Then look over your shoulder
and you just might see
someone else smiling at you—
and maybe it might be me.

20

Get on Board

Story-quilt by **Cheryl Willis Hudson**

The words to this popular song are sung in classrooms all across
the United States. You can just open your mouth and sing along.
There's room for many more!

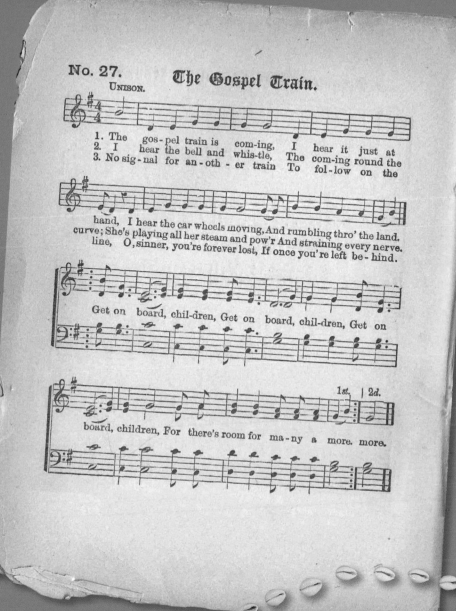

The fare is cheap and all can go,
The rich and poor are there,
No second-class on board the train,
No difference in the fare.

Facsimile page taken from
THE STORY OF THE JUBILEE SINGERS WITH THEIR SONGS, *revised edition, 1881*

You Can Change the World

Bernette G. Ford   Illustration by **George Ford**

When I was growing up in the 1960s, the Civil Rights Movement was in the news every night. My sister and I saw black people on television, our people in the South, protesting unfair laws and demonstrating against the white people and the government that enforced those laws. They were being beaten by white police officers, and hosed and chased by vicious dogs, and shot at (and even killed) for the right to vote, or to go to the school of their choice, or to eat at any lunch counter. In 1963, four little black girls were killed when a bomb placed by racist white men blew up in their church in Birmingham, Alabama, while they were going to Sunday school. Up here in the North, our Sunday school sponsored a group of young civil rights workers, little more than children themselves, to come to Long Island, New York, in 1963 for a few weeks without conflict and fear and stress.

My parents volunteered to open our home to a young girl, not much older than my sister Lisa and I (I think I was twelve or thirteen), who was demonstrating for her rights down South. She needed a respite from all the hate and cruelty and violence she was experiencing at the hands of hateful white folks almost every day at home.

Debby stayed with us for a week or two, and during that time, we got to know her and love her. She inspired us with her bravery and her stories and her spirit and her determination to fight until she won justice for the black people in her town and all over the South.

When Debby went back home, we worried. Lisa and I had terrible nightmares. We felt like the world was coming to an end. The peace we had always counted on was gone. We were terrified that our new friend Debby, or some of her friends or family, might be killed. We felt like there was nothing we could do. We felt helpless . . . and hopeless.

But then our mother and father told us we must never give up hope. They encouraged us to act. There were many things we could do, and we found that our actions gave us hope. We wrote letters to newspapers; we wrote reports about civil rights for school and hung them on the bulletin board. We wrote to the president of the United States. If we couldn't write, we drew pictures and made posters. We demonstrated and marched alongside family and friends in New York City. We chanted and sang freedom songs. We prayed. We made enough noise that our voices could be heard, and we turned the energy of fear and hopelessness into action to make changes in the laws used to discriminate against black people.

When you are working with people who believe in changing the world, you *can* change the world. No matter how dark or scary or hateful the times, there are always more good people in the world than bad. It took a while, but we won back then with the passing of the Civil Rights Act of 1964. This Civil Rights Act became the law of our country, and it guaranteed that all black people would have the same rights as whites. It ended discrimination because of race, color, religion, sex, or national origin. It meant that black people of all ages in the South could go to any school or live in any neighborhood or be served at any restaurant or use any public restroom they wanted to.

When we raise our voices whenever we see something that needs to be changed in the world, when we raise them against injustice, it inspires other people to do the same thing. Then you will see just how many people are on your side! The power of all our voices becomes stronger and louder. And that can only happen when people start to act and inspire others to do the same!

The good people won one civil rights battle back in 1964. But the fight is not over. Somehow bad people do come back to scare us or hurt us. So we have to keep working

ART IN THREE DIMENSIONS
Bernette
SMITH STREET SCHOOL
UNIONDALE L I
MRS DE LUCA
GRADE 5
APRIL 1961

and fighting in our own way. Even now, we have to keep up the fight for people to be treated fairly no matter if they are rich or poor, for all people to have affordable medical care, for people to be able to practice their religion free from fear of harm. And if we do that, if we take action to change the world, then we can surely win again.

Next

Lesa Cline-Ransome
Illustration by **James E. Ransome**

She grew up in the cotton
  fields of North Carolina
at her mother's hip, in her
  father's footsteps
sprouting tall and strong
among the stalks
in southern sun and soil

Her head bent, her back
  curved
as she dragged a sack
  behind her
blinking away dust,
  breathing in dirt
she chopped and picked
  soft fluff out of sharp
  bolls
that drew blood

She bit her tongue when
  her daddy was told on
  settling day
after months of bending
  and picking
*You'll do better next
  season*
But *next season* don't fill
  empty pockets
  or hungry bellies
standing eye to eye with
  her mama and papa
in the dark of night, she
  whispered goodbye,
  headed north
the next train

The sun rose on a city
  budding tall buildings
fast walkers and loud cars
while hatred beat down on
  her neck
and fear blew in her face

she worked still from
  sunup to sundown
on a factory line clocking
  in one day
after the next
hoping to make something
  beautiful blossom from
  nothing

She scratched and scraped
away the next years
and watched as
Martin
Malcolm
Fannie
Ella
Rosa
Medgar
Ruby
Al
took the next steps

Watched as they
preached
marched
sat
stood
boycotted
sued
and voted
giving birth to a new crop
the next generation
built tall and strong
to brave the winds of hate
   and ignorance
her back straightened, her
   eyes widened
her voice grew louder
and she began planting her
   own seeds up one row
down the next

at home
in schools
in pews
in voting booths
her vote counted through
   one president
after the next
Kennedy
Johnson
Nixon
Ford
Carter
Reagan
Bush
Clinton
Bush
from Obama
she sowed hope,
   reaped courage
from rain and drought

In a world that says
Wait
Not now
Next season
she stands in footprints left in
   the soil of those who came
   before
and those who will come next
who will never wither under
   the rockiest dirt, the
   hottest sun
the scores of weevils
she tills the soil for her
   people
who keep growing tall and
   strong through

the next day
the next week
the next month
the next vote
the next election
the next president

29

Drumbeat for Change

Kelly Starling Lyons

This world feels upside down sometimes,
like a twisted house of mirrors where
    people in charge are bullies,
where protestors of racism are pummeled,
where being who you are can put your
    life on the line.
What do we do with the worry, the hurt,
    the rage?
We turn it into something bigger than us.
We turn it into change.

Together, we are a mountain
    no one can destroy.
Having faith doesn't mean we are fearless.
It means we believe and press on.
Toward love.
Toward equality.
Toward a safer, stronger future.
We press on and stay true to what
    we know is right.

Throughout history, kids like you
    were right there.
With picket signs and petitions.
With heart and humility.
With bravery and brilliance.
They changed this world for the better.
And you will too.

Tell your story.
To anyone who will listen.
To hear it yourself.

You matter.
You *matter*.
You. Matter.
The drumbeat of hope will always
    drown out howls of hate.

Can you hear it?
Can you feel it?
Say it with me and believe.
I matter.
I *matter*.
I. Matter.
Beautiful you.
I am in awe.
Of all you are and will be.

When you feel angry or afraid,
    remember what you hold inside.
Kindness.
Courage.
Compassion.
The power of people who made
    a way out of no way.
Who persevered and toppled injustice.
Live in you.
Always.

March to that drumbeat of hope.
March and know you are never alone.
Standing up and speaking out,
pressing for justice,
having each other's backs,
we will create change.

Dr. Martin Luther King Jr. is shown leading a group of black children to their newly integrated school in Grenada, Mississippi. They are escorted by folk singer Joan Baez and two of Dr. King's aides, Rev. Andrew Young (left) and Rev. Hosea Williams (next to Baez).

The Art of Mindfulness

Evelyn Coleman   Photograph by **Zamani Feelings**

Even though you're a child, remember you are the future of our world. When I was a child, my father taught me that the heart of the living earth was in me and every living being. He reminded me to think about that whenever I felt anger toward someone. This is called the art of "mindfulness."

If you were to put your ear to the ground, you too would hear the earth's heartbeat. Now hold your hand over your heart, be very still, and listen; you'll hear that same beat inside you. That beat is also inside every living person on earth. Sometimes you'll forget it's there, as many people have forgotten. People who no longer remember they have the same heart as others are mean to them, hurt them, and only care about themselves. But just because one person forgets doesn't mean we all should forget. We must all remember, and that begins with you.

Don't think this means you can never be mad or feel sad or disappointed with someone. In fact, we need to understand our feelings because they help us figure out the world. However, not all feelings are real. For instance, we might feel scared of something that hasn't even happened or may never happen. The important thing to remember is that feelings are signals that make us think and make us mindful. Think about when you did something you shouldn't have. When asked why you did it, you responded, "I don't know." When you examine your feelings before you act on them, you will learn not to make the same mistake.

If you don't examine your feelings and your responses to them, it will be much harder to become a "mindful" human being. Becoming mindful is one of the most important jobs on this earth. It means paying attention to how you are living in the world. You are here to bless the earth and to honor your creation. I know that you will grow up to be a person who understands how important it is to protect yourself and those around you, to plant the seeds of peace wherever you go. If each of us does our part, imagine how beautiful a world we would have almost instantly.

A step in that direction is to make a friend with someone from another race, culture, or ethnic group. I don't mean just sit with them at school or play with them on the playground. I mean go home with them and get to know their family, and invite them to your home to know your family. Sometimes it is not possible to do this if you happen to be in a family that doesn't want to be with people who are different. But you could do it when you're older. Once you engage in this way, you will appreciate how our differences make us richer, healthier, smarter, and more empathetic. Think about it. If every child made friends this way, we would have a more peaceful and accepting world. In less than twenty years, the world would be filled with people who are as mindful as you, who also hear the heartbeat of others.

One Day Papí Drove Me to School

Tony Medina   Illustrations by **Edel Rodriguez**

1 One day Papí drove me to school
Like he always does, talking about my homework:
Science, History and Math. He made a funny face
When I told him all I had to add.
Lots of kids were in front of the building and others were being dropped off.
I turned to Papí to ask him, "Will you pick me up after school?"
And before I knew it, four cops came running toward him.
I heard a commotion, looked to my right and screamed, *"Papí! Papí!"*
I saw my papí go down on the ground, tackled and shackled and
Hands cuffed behind his back.

I could not see Papí's face; the cop with his knee on Papí's back smashed it into the
pavement as he grabbed a fistful of Papí's hair. All I could see were Papí's jeans and his
construction boots.

I screamed. The world started to sweep from beneath my feet and buildings started
to tumble and I nearly had an asthma attack from my constant screams. One cop—a
woman with the word *ICE* on her back—pulled me by my waist as I flailed and kicked in
desperation.

Students, parents, and some teachers crowded around as the officers held me to the
ground, while my papí was pushed into a police van.

"La Migra! La Migra!" someone yelled. Others laughed with their fat-fish faces, taunt-
ing me with "Alien" and "Illegal" and "Get out!" and "Go back to your country!"

I shouted, *"This IS my country, you stupid doofus heads!"*

Before I knew it, a crowd of white kids surrounded me, but other kids, black and
brown and some white, came to my rescue. Somehow, though, *I* was the one who was
taken to the principal's office!

2 Now the school was split in half.

A crazy group of kids wore **Make America Great Again** hats, just to taunt us.

But others, black, brown, and white kids, were down with us—and not racism!

In all my nine years on the planet, I never had a fight! But a handful of kids wanted to start trouble. One day they scrunched up their faces and balled up their fists. We stepped forward in unison. We took off our jackets and our sweaters and dropped them to the ground. Then we stuck out our chests real proud, so they could see our T-shirts that read:

I AM NOT AN ALIEN.

I AM NOT ILLEGAL.

WHY DON'T YOU GO BACK TO YOUR OWN COUNTRY?

IS NOT MY FAVORITE SONG

GET OUT!

IS NOT MY NAME.

NO MORE BORDERS.

NO MORE WALLS.

3 The bullies backed down that day and moved on to their classrooms.

The next day, the **Make America Great Again** hats had disappeared.

Instead, some kids asked, "Where can I get the cool T-shirts?"

We didn't get any more glares or stares.

One of the boys who bullied me even came up to me and said, "My mom's a lawyer; she can help your dad!"

And as we walked to our class, he turned to me. "Guess what?"

I said, "What?"

"I'm just like you."

I gave him the side-eye and answered back, "A girl?"

He laughed and I laughed, and then he said, "My father's from Croatia."

4 That would make the perfect ending—for a movie!
But this is real life, and they took my papí away.
And once again the world was swept from under my feet—and Mamí's!
She has to find a new job to help take care of us and help get Papí back.

One day my papí drove me to school.
A day I'll never forget.
I get sad and scared when I think about where Papí is.
I keep his photo in the gold locket he gave me last Christmas.
I keep it pressed tight and close to my heart.

It Helps to Look at Old Front Page Headlines

Marilyn Nelson   iPadology by **Mansa K. Mussa**

The earthquakes, the militias. History
hairpins and switchbacks like a mountain road.
Things fall apart, no doubt. But good people wake
every day to thank, and to ask what they can do
today to make things better. People call
things back together when they choose to act
on behalf of our planet and all life
spinning with us on her around the sun.

Worrying only wastes our limited time
and darkens our skies with cumulonimbus clouds.
All we can do is hold faith and go on
leaving our tiny footprints on history.
Today's acts of good will change tomorrow.
Good is, good is in control, and good will win.

All Nations Are Neighbors and I Wonder

Margarita Engle   Illustration by **Rafael López**

All Nations Are Neighbors

Deep
beneath sea waves
and high above
on aerial flyways
fish, turtles, and birds
visit each other's homelands
swiftly
while the rest of us
have learned to wait
patiently
finding our own written pathways
by sending slow words
of encouragement
back and forth
sweet
echoes
of friendship.

I Wonder

Does a butterfly miss
its wiggly caterpillar days?

Do tadpoles suspect
that they'll soon grow four
jumpy legs?

How does the leafy future
of an immense green tree
fit inside this tiny
seed?

I don't know, but I'm going to plant
many seedlings anyway, so that by the time
I'm old, a whole forest will wave
happy branches.

When I Think of You

Sharon G. Flake Photographs by **Zamani Feelings**

How are you, my love? Well, I hope. I've been thinking about you lately. So, I wanted to check in, to make sure you're okay. I see you … draped in confidence, walking like you own the world, looking fine, skateboarding, protesting injustice, helping out friends. My heart sings at the thought of what is possible for us here on earth because you exist. What I admire about you most is your smile, your ability to make jokes in nearly any situation, and just how creative and entrepreneurial you are. I didn't have your courage and tenacity when I was young. Everything scared me—boys, taking risks, being judged. Yet, here I am. I made it through all my personal trials and tribulations, the world's too. You will also. Count on it.

But know this—the world is larger than your school and neighborhood, crazier than ever, it seems. Has it gotten you down, made you feel as if you aren't as brave or in control as you once thought you were? If so, I understand. We had the Vietnam War and discrimination. My dad had Jim Crow, the Depression, and World War II.

Every generation faces a series of storms that seem insurmountable. Your generation is no different. The internet and cable news stream reports to us nightly: Another black boy shot and killed by the police. Families torn apart as parents get deported. Swastikas and nooses peppering our landscape like weeds. Adults berating and brawling with their neighbors and constituents. Even the climate seems discontent, determined to bring out the worst in us all.

Thankfully, it is in the nature of youth to look at the landscape, no matter how charred and forlorn, and see new growth, new opportunity, and visions of possibilities. Do you still see what is possible? What's good and everlasting despite the times and conditions we live in? Do you understand how important you and other youth are to us?

When I think of you, I think of those who have come before you. Young and resilient, they lived during history's most tumultuous times and left their mark. Muhammad Ali, formerly Cassius Clay, was one of them. At twelve, he was an amateur boxer. By eighteen, he was an Olympic gold medalist who later raised his fists against injustice. Malala Yousafzai, from Pakistan, was shot by terrorists who didn't think girls should attend school. At seventeen, Malala won a Nobel Peace Prize for her bravery and efforts to educate girls. There are others like you three. Ordinary citizens like these. Alicia Garza, cofounder of Black Lives Matter. Emmett Till, brutally murdered for allegedly whistling at a white woman. His death launched the civil rights era. Anne Frank, whose diary of her Holocaust experiences and continued faith in mankind impacted millions. Claudette Colvin, who refused to give a white person her seat on the bus.

And William Kamkwamba, who at the age of fourteen built a windmill to power his parents' home in Malawi, Africa. Because of William, his family and village had running water and electricity for the first time.

Hard times do not always harden people. Often, they reveal what we're made of—who we are inside. I believe *you* are amazing. That if you take care of yourself and your heart, you will add much value to the planet in your own special way. So again I ask, how are you? Are you having fun during these tough times? Are you serving others while being kind and concerned about yourself? Good, because I need you to know you are loved. You are needed. And you were born for such a time as this.

Blessings on your journey,
Your fan and cheerleader,
Sharon G. Flake

a day of small things

Tonya Bolden Illustration by **Vanessa Brantley-Newton**

have a day of small things:
compliment someone on an outfit
   or hairdo,
congratulate a friend on a victory,
gift a stranger with a smile,
telephone—don't text—an elder
   in the family,
give a few dollars to a worthy cause,
spend fifteen minutes—cell phone off—
   thinking about
someone other than yourself:
a soul who has suffered a loss,
   a heartbreak,
someone in need of a favor
or cheering up
or a surprise.

write a gentle poem.

no one becomes a
a bully
a grouch
self-centered soul
vulgar
overnight.
bit
by
bit—that's how it happens:

a snicker here,
a chuckle there at a mean-spirited joke,
a passing on of gossip to itching ears.

so it is with growing into goodness.

bit
by
bit.

if you make a habit of
having just one day a week
of small things
you may find that
Generosity
Reciprocity
Agape love
Compassion
Empathy
become second nature,
your way of life,
who
you
truly
are
inside.

Dark-Brown Skin Is Beautiful

Eleanora E. Tate   Photograph by **Chester Higgins Jr.**

In my novel *Thank You, Dr. Martin Luther King, Jr.!* fourth-grader Mary Elouise Avery is dark-skinned. Not "dark-skinned" like mega singers Beyoncé and Nicki Minaj. Dark-skinned like actresses Lupita Nyong'o and Viola Davis. And writers like me.

Dark-brown skin is beautiful. Know it. Claim it. Yet too many dark-brown-skinned girls are bullied and ridiculed. Mary Elouise Avery wishes that she has "pinkish-tan" skin, like her new white classmate Brandy has, or at least light-brown skin, like her nemesis Libby Burns has. Mary Elouise's mother has even called her an "ugly ole Black thing."

You can try to defend yourself from other kids by fighting back with words or fists or trying to ignore the dark-skin verbal abuse. But when your own relatives in your own home call you "ugly Black thing," "charcoal," "blue Black," "ruint," "crow," and worse names, what can a kid do?

Sometimes relatives defend their insults by saying such name-calling is "keeping it real" or that this verbal abuse will "toughen you up." Yeah, right.

My mother and sister were light-brown-skinned. Mother would say, "We never held it against you that you were dark." Well, thanks. But my mother would also say, "You're so dark. Your face is so greasy. People don't like dark, greasy colored girls." Because I was "so dark," she said I couldn't accomplish anything that girls of lighter hue could. So I shouldn't even try. It didn't matter that I was smarter and had more ambition than many of them.

I learned something from my experiences. By the time I turned fifteen, I had developed a simple, secret, radical plan to get away from my mother's perpetual "dark skin" beat-down. I claimed the beauty of my dark skin. I studied hard. I got a little part-time job. I saved my money. I learned practical skills. I cried a lot, but I kept on trying.

By the end of my book, Mary Elouise Avery learns from her experiences, too. Although she is still young, she learns about skin color and self-esteem. "We have to learn to be our own best friends first," her dark-skinned grandmother Big Momma tells her, "and do what we can to work on being good to ourselves."

This is my hope for you: Be good to yourself! Keep loving your dark skin. Prepare for your present and your future by affirming your self-worth now—not based on skin color or any other superficial or shallow or physical standards, but rather affirm it in the words of Dr. Martin Luther King Jr., who said:

"I have a dream that my four little children will one day live in a nation where they will not be judged by the color of their skin but by the content of their character."

If you can survive your relatives' in-home bullying about your skin color, you will surely survive out in the world, I did.

here is a poem of love and hope:

Arnold Adoff

from a cold
de cem ber
a f t e r n o o n
out here in the flatland of e a s t ohio
and i am o u t in this considerable yard
u n d e r this h e a v y grey sky
pres s i ng on to my s h o u l d e r s
and s w e e t w o m a n
my head is bending l o w as the song goes
and my eyes are fixed on frozen patches of past
and future loves and deaths and dis re gards
and i am l i v i n g into my eight i eth y e a r
and i still address these poems to you to y o u r
eyes to that always welcoming smile to those
w e l c o m i n g   a r m s

i am stripping away all that is not   necessary
and this has been my p l a n m y pro cess
for m o s t of my conscious l i f e out here
discerning what is alive and what is   almost
worth the mouth to mouth of the h e a r t
and i still believe in the power and force of love
as i can almost feel the land s h a k i n g with
the power and force of mindful des truc t i o n
and   i   shake under the daily drumbeat of death

please r e a d this poem with your o w n power and l o v e
and smile and r e r e a d and nod and be angry with resolve
these s t r u g g l e s must continue through h a r d w i n t e r
as we prepare for the new and g r e e n i n g s p r i n g

We've Got You

Pat Cummings

The storm is coming.
There is always a storm
But we've got you.
We've weathered the fury
you're heading into.
And we know how to shelter.
How to gather force.
We've seen where the storm
  is weak.
We've got you.

So tuck in,
    stay close,
        grow strong.
We're here. Your wind.

And you?
        You're our coming storm.

How to Pass the Test

Hena Khan Photographs by **Stephan J. Hudson**

If they call you a "Muzzlam," spitting out the word at you, it will probably upset you. It might make you wonder why it sounds like an insult. But they are not only mispronouncing the word *Muslim*. They are misunderstanding the 1.6 billion peace-loving, ice-cream-eating, cartoon-watching Muslim people like you and me living in every corner of the globe.

Tell them that a Muslim (emphasizing how to say it correctly) is a person who practices the religion of Islam. And that, like most religions, Islam is rooted in love, discipline, and striving to be a good person.

If they say "go home," curling their lips with anger, it will probably hurt you. It might make you wonder where in the world you could go, if you even wanted to. This *is* your home, and you have as much of a right to be here as anybody else. People in America are united by the freedom to practice their religion, whatever it is.

Tell them that Muslims have been part of our country since its very beginning, and that we've been here for centuries. We helped build this country and shape it into what it is today—from the cotton fields to the factories to the front lines to the hospitals to the class-rooms. We love our country, and we are here to stay.

If they call you "terrorist," pointing their fingers at you, it will probably disgust you. It might frighten you to think of the evil people doing terrible things in the name of your religion. But terrorists are nothing like you. Violent extremists of any kind don't represent what you or 99.9 percent of Muslims believe. Just like the Ku Klux Klan doesn't reflect all Christians.

Tell them that hatred and ignorance of all types fuel craziness. And that includes bullying and discrimination against innocent Muslims right here. You are not at fault for the twisted actions of others. You have done nothing wrong.

But if they call you a "friend," offering to protect you and to stand by you, it

will comfort you. It might make you feel less alone and scared. These are the people who take the time to learn about others beyond headlines, to find common ground, and to understand. These are the people who reject the hate mongers and bigots. These are the majority of Americans, who share the same values as Muslims and remember the struggles of others—of other religions, other races, other ethnicities—for equality and freedom.

Tell them you are grateful for their friendship. Join them in the cause of fairness and goodness and kindness, toward all people, of all backgrounds and faiths. Stay strong. Be proud of who you are. This is a test, and it isn't easy. But it will pass.

Where Are the Good People?

Tameka Fryer Brown   Illustration by **Innosanto Nagara**

Life's not always fair
and sometimes it's scary.
When safe spaces aren't safe,
when protectors harm us,
when leaders try to lead us
toward fear and hate,
there's nothing fair
or reassuring about that.

Maybe it would be helpful to know
these aren't the first
troubling times
our world has seen,
that none has ever lasted
forever.

Tyrants rise and fall;
bad guys win,
then lose;
evil gets
overtaken by good
when good people stand together
against it.

Who and where are the good people?

They're all around us
every day
telling truths,
seeking justice,
persisting.
They are the helpers,
the listeners,
the lovers of everyone.

There are more good people
than not.
They will win.
We will win
if we believe
and don't get tired of believing.

Changemakers—
that's what they'll call us
tomorrows from now
if you and I
fight for fairness
starting today.
Do you believe that we can?
I do too.
Action is power . . .

Let's get to work!

You Can Do It

Jabari Asim   *Photo collage by* **Nina Crews**

You can do it,
No matter what they say.
You can learn and love and grow
Each and every day.

You can do it,
Though others may think not.
Put your back into it,
Give it everything you've got.

Any dream can happen,
The world is yours to win.
It doesn't matter where you're from
Or the color of your skin.

Bullies may try to stop you
And say you don't belong
But they will never top you
And you will prove them wrong.

Your ancestors came across the waters
And made a life in this new land.
Mighty sons and daughters,
The future is in your hands.

You can do it with magic and thunder.
You can do it with rhythm and skill.
You can do it with wisdom and wonder.
You can do it, and you will.

Tell It in Your Own Way

Roy Boney Jr.

I am a full-blood Cherokee artist from a small town called Locust Grove, Oklahoma. I have been drawing as long as I can remember. Growing up, I used to watch a lot of cartoons and read lots of comic books. Now that I'm an adult, I still do! As a kid, I spent hours trying to draw what I saw on-screen and on the page. Sometimes I would get in trouble because I was drawing in class and the teachers thought I wasn't paying attention. Doodling helped me focus on what the teacher was saying even if I appeared to not be listening.

I grew up in a family where many people spoke the Cherokee language. I never thought it was unique until I got older and realized that my experience as a Native American was different from a lot of the other kids. No one in my family had gone to college, so I never gave that much thought, either. I thought of drawing only as a hobby. Fortunately, one of my art teachers saw how much I loved drawing. He encouraged me to consider going to college to study art.

At first I resisted. I didn't think I needed an education in art. Also, because I was a Cherokee kid who liked to draw, a lot of people told me that I should be painting pictures of Native Americans the way they were portrayed in old western movies. I didn't like that kind of imagery because as a modern Cherokee, those types of images didn't express what my life was like. My family never ran around in buckskins, and we never lived in tipis. We drove cars, lived in houses, and watched TV like everybody else. And we laughed a lot! If I was going to make art, it would be art that I enjoyed and that expressed my experience as a Cherokee person living in the modern era.

This is one of my favorite illustrations. The actual piece is called *Simpquoyah,* and it is a cartoonized version of Sequoyah based on a popular television illustration style. *Simpquoyah* is drawn as a digital vector illustration, so it can be published to scale at any size and resolution. The caption in the drawing is written in Cherokee and translates as "Do you understand Cherokee?" The background is made up of the Cherokee syllabary as originally designed by Sequoyah himself. In the corner is my signature written in Cherokee. This is one of my favorite pieces because it combines several loves of mine: the Cherokee language, humor, cartoons, and digital illustration. While I do lots of painting and drawing, I enjoy creating digital artwork. My formal training is in graphic design and illustration, so the medium is fun for me.

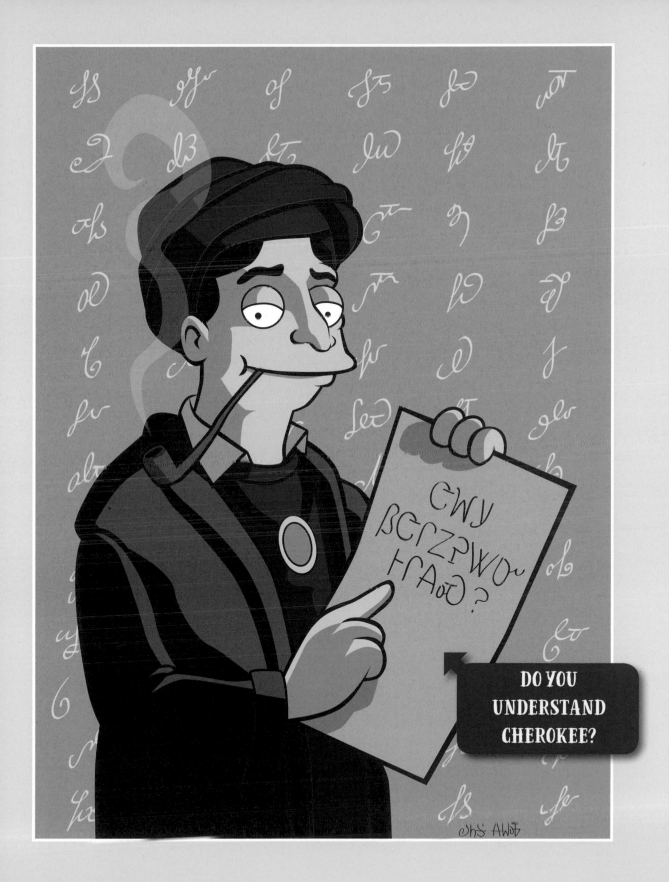

So with the support of my family and help from my art teacher, I applied to college and studied graphic design. I learned how to use computers to do illustration and animation and make websites. I have since received my bachelor's degree and my master's degree in art. After I graduated, I started publishing comic books, making animations in the Cherokee language, and entering fine art competitions that featured my own version of modern Cherokee art.

A Cherokee man named Sequoyah invented a way to write the Cherokee language in 1821. It is called the Cherokee syllabary, and I use it a lot in my artwork. It helps teach others the language and educates people about Cherokee culture. This kid from a small town in Oklahoma has since had art shown in Paris, London, and Italy, and across the United States. Why? Because I chose to not follow stereotypes and to express my own story through my art. Every person has his or her own story, but it's up to you to tell it in your own way.

This digital image is based on an original portrait of Sequoyah painted by Charles Bird King in 1828. In my digital rendering, Sequoyah is holding an iPad, but the original syllabary was written in longhand with a quill pen. Over time, print and typeset characters evolved for practical use via printing presses and computer keyboards.

Members of the Young People's Chorus of New York City

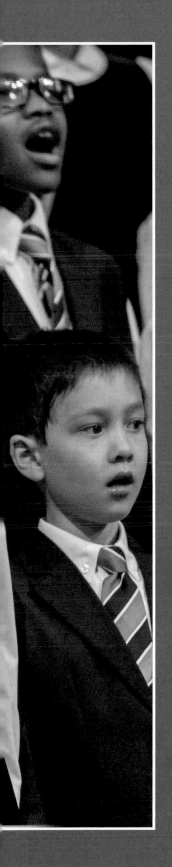

What Songs Will Our Children Sing?

Curtis Hudson   Photograph by **Stephanie Berger**

What songs will our children sing to their children?
What melodies will softly put them to sleep?
Will they sing songs to make them dream of a brighter future?
Will the stories they tell give them hope and bring them peace?

The world is out of tune and so out of rhythm.
So much hate and confusion fill our nation.
We just can't sit back; we must work to find a solution.
So there will be a new dance and a new song
      for a new generation.

What songs will our children sing to their children?
Will the lyrics ring out love, or will
      they loudly ring out the sounds of hate?
Will there be songs that tell of wars and destruction?
Or will there be songs that shout of victory
      to make them celebrate?

The world could be a beautiful place,
But we must start now, there is no time, no time to waste.
We must bring, bring back love and harmony
So there'll be freedom for the world and hope for all humanity.

How will they find their way if there is no one to lead them?
There must be a better way, but they need someone
      to teach them
That love is our only hope to change the world
So our children will be free, every boy and girl.

What songs will our children sing to their children?
What inspiration will they find in the words?
The songs that our children sing to their children
Will be the songs we teach our children to sing.

You Too Can Fly

Zetta Elliott Illustration by Laura Freeman

do not forget
  to marvel
at the wonders
of the world

when sinister
  shadows gather
and fear clutches
your tender heart
remember:
the fiercest dragons
emerge from the
  darkest depths
and a single star
  sparkling
in the sable sky
may guide you to
your destiny

when others attempt
to school you
in the ways of cruelty
learn lessons from
Aesop's clever crow
open your
third eye
to see past the ruins
and envision
a better world

when the struggle
  to survive
leaves you breathless
know that we
have outpaced
  hounds
and tunneled through
  mountains of
  despair
to emerge unbowed
and free

the whip could not
  break us
the noose could not
  choke our joy

when our ancestors
had no cheek left to
  turn
they walked into
  the sea
or stepped into
  the sky

remember:
you too
can
fly

Advice . . . (I'm Old-School Like That)

Olugbemisola Rhuday-Perkovich

I know I'm old-school. My parents, both immigrants, valued good manners and respect for elders. So do I. I also went to many different schools throughout childhood, and being the New Kid many times over meant that my best bet was to keep my mouth shut and figure things out if I wanted to get it right. I want things to be right for you. I want you to be safe. I want your way to be smooth.

But I learned that more important than getting it "right" is understanding how many times I'll get it wrong. I know that I'll be knocked down and need to get up again, over and over. I know there is beauty and power in the learning, the making of mistakes, the taking of risks, and living my life "like it's golden."

I give advice knowing that there is much I need to get, to learn, to do, and do over. I give advice knowing that I love you.

I give advice knowing that this is a world roiling with pain and fear and anger and hurt . . . and love. I give advice even though I am afraid. I give advice even though I have no idea what I'm doing.

But I know that I love you.

- ☀ YOUR VOICE IS PRECIOUS, AND IT MATTERS.
- ☀ KNOW THAT YOU MIGHT HAVE TO REMIND ME OF THAT SOMETIMES.
- ☀ BECAUSE I'M OLD-SCHOOL LIKE THAT.
- ☀ LISTEN, AND LISTEN AGAIN.
- ☀ LOVING AND CELEBRATING YOURSELF IS NOT RACIST, AND YOU SHOULD DO IT AT LEAST ONCE A DAY.
- ☀ READ, AND READ WIDELY.
- ☀ ASK QUESTIONS, AND NEVER ASSUME YOU HAVE ALL THE ANSWERS.
- ☀ TAKE ALL THE TIME AND ALL THE SPACE YOU NEED.
- ☀ READ, AND READ WIDELY.
- ☀ TAKE THE OPPORTUNITY TO AMPLIFY THE VOICES OF THE OPPRESSED AND MARGINALIZED.
- ☀ USE YOUR VOICE IN THE WAY YOU SEE FIT, AND NOT IN THE WAY THAT OTHERS, INCLUDING ME, TELL YOU IS THE "RIGHT" WAY TO DO IT.
- ☀ YOU MIGHT HAVE TO REMIND ME OF THAT ONE TOO.

* KNOW THAT SPEAKING TRUTH TO POWER IN LOVE IS NEVER WORTHLESS, EVEN IF OTHERS DON'T SEEM TO HEAR YOU.
* KNOW THAT SOMETIMES SILENCE SPEAKS LIKE A PIERCING SHOUT.
* LOVE AND CHERISH AND CARE FOR YOURSELF.
* LOVE AND CHERISH AND CARE FOR SOMEONE ELSE.
* ASK QUESTIONS, AND NEVER ASSUME YOU HAVE ALL THE ANSWERS.
* LISTEN, AND LISTEN AGAIN.
* CREATE, MAKE ART, TELL YOUR STORY.
* READ, AND READ WIDELY.
* KNOW THAT NO ONE ELSE CAN DEFINE YOU.
* YOU ARE NOT RESPONSIBLE FOR OTHERS' IGNORANCE OR HATE.
* YOU CAN ALWAYS BE RESPECTFUL WITHOUT WORRYING ABOUT BEING NICE.

- ☀ YOU HAVE EVERY RIGHT TO SMILE, AND ENJOY WHO YOU ARE.
- ☀ YOU DON'T HAVE TO SMILE.
- ☀ LISTEN, AND LISTEN AGAIN.
- ☀ READ, AND READ WIDELY.
- ☀ KNOW THAT YOUR LIFE IS A TRIUMPH; YOU ARE A LUMINOUS THREAD IN A GORGEOUSLY WOVEN TAPESTRY OF LOVE, STRUGGLE, AND VIBRANT STORY.
- ☀ KNOW THAT THERE IS MUSIC—DRUMS AND HYMNS, BLUES AND BEATS, ROCK AND ROLL AND ON AND ON AND ON—IN YOUR BLOOD.
- ☀ ASK QUESTIONS, AND NEVER ASSUME YOU HAVE ALL THE ANSWERS.
- ☀ WHO YOU ARE, AT THE VERY CORE OF YOUR SOUL, IS BEAUTIFUL.
- ☀ YOUR VOICE IS PRECIOUS, AND IT MATTERS.
- ☀ TELL YOUR STORY.

AND REMEMBER THAT I LOVE YOU.

A Talkin'-To

Jason Reynolds Illustration by **Andrea Pippins**

I could tell you all the bad things,
all the bad things that cut and scare
and howl and growl and gnash and
bear teeth, bright and sharp that
glint in the moonlight.

I could tell you all that's frightening,
all that's frightening and lurking
and looming and hiding in the brush,
razor-hair pricked up on the back
of something too sly to see.

I could tell you about all the loud things,
all the loud things that scream
and shriek and shred our ability to hear
each other, the beasts behind screens,
scrolling banners of bully-banter.

I could tell you all the things,
all the things that are trying to tell you
about you, about how you should run,
and how you should run,
and how you should run,
but I'm about you above all things,
above all things, so I'd rather tell you
one thing and one thing only:

everything bad and frightening and loud
will always hide when you hold your head up,
will always hide when you hold your heart out,
will always sing a shrinking song
when you fly.

About the Contributors

 **Arnold Adoff** is a poet and anthologist for young readers and their older allies... //

he has published more than forty books since 1968... received the ncte award for the body of his work... as well as many other honors....

he will always be married to the genius african american novelist and folklorist... virginia esther hamilton adoff... and is one of the leaders of the virginia hamilton conference on multicultural literature for youth... held each year at kent state university in ohio... and is deeply involved in the arnold adoff poetry awards given at the conference.... //

he has created his own synthesis of music and meaning... a style of shaped colloquial speech... and entering his eightieth year on the planet... is p o e t i n g with energies and control... while struggling within the tyranny of chronology... and the daily drumbeat of death and destruction.... //
arnoldadoff.com | poetandonewomanband.com

 **Kwame Alexander** is a poet, an educator, and a *New York Times* bestselling author. He has written twenty-four books, including *Rebound*, the prequel to *The Crossover*, his middle-grade novel that received the John Newbery Medal for the Most Distinguished Contribution to American Literature for Children, the Coretta Scott King Author Award Honor, the NCTE Charlotte Huck Honor, the Lee Bennett Hopkins Poetry Award, and the Paterson Poetry Prize. Some of his other works include *The Playbook: 52 Rules to Help You Aim, Shoot, and Score in This Game of Life*, the picture books *Animal Ark* and *Out of Wonder*, and the YA novel *Solo*.

The recipient of the inaugural Pat Conroy Legacy Award, Kwame believes that poetry can change the world, and he uses it to inspire and empower young people through his Writing Workshop. Recently, he led a delegation of twenty writers and activists to Ghana, where they delivered books, built a library, and provided literacy professional development to 300 teachers as part of LEAP for Ghana, an international literacy program he cofounded. Kwame is the host of the literary variety/talk show *Bookish*, which airs on Wednesdays on Facebook Watch.
kwamealexander.com

 **Jabari Asim** is an associate professor at Emerson College, where he directs the graduate program in creative writing. He is the author of thirteen books, including *Preaching to the Chickens: The Story of Young John Lewis; Fifty Cents and a Dream: Young Booker T. Washington; Whose Toes Are Those?* and *Girl of Mine.*

His reviews, essays, and cultural criticism have been published in the *New York Times*, the *Wall Street Journal*, *USA Today*, the *Los Angeles Times*, the *Village Voice*, the *Boston Globe*, the *Washington Post*, and *Essence*, among others.

His honors include a Guggenheim Fellowship for Creative Arts, the Carter G. Woodson Book Award from the National Council for the Social Studies, and a Jefferson Cup Honor from the Virginia Library Association.
therealjabariasim.com

Stephanie Berger has been photographing performance and cultural events for over twenty-five years for such major cultural centers as Lincoln Center, the Brooklyn Academy of Music, Carnegie Hall, the Metropolitan Museum of Art, the Dia Art Foundation, and the Baryshnikov Arts Center.

She has been the staff photographer for the Lincoln Center Festival since its inception in 1996. Berger has been commissioned by many top dance companies, theater companies, and musicians, including Merce Cunningham, Bill T. Jones, and New York City's Young People's Chorus. She works regularly for PBS, photographing many of their hosts, and has exhibited her photographs in major galleries and public art spaces.

Berger graduated from the University of Massachusetts at Amherst and studied photography with Jerome Liebling at Hampshire College. She worked as a photographer for the City of New York's Department of Transportation in the 1980s, documenting New York City's infrastructure and public works. She is also a member of the 52nd Street Project.
stephaniebergerphoto.com

Tonya Bolden, author, editor, and coauthor of more than forty books, is a recipient of the Children's Book Guild of Washington, DC's Nonfiction Award for her body of work. Bolden's books include *Maritcha: A Nineteenth-Century American Girl,* a Coretta Scott King Honor Book and James Madison Book Award winner, and *M.L.K.: Journey of a King,* winner of an NCTE Orbis Pictus Award.

Bolden's *Searching for Sarah Rector: The Richest Black Girl in America* received several starred reviews. Said *Kirkus:* "Bolden admirably tells a complex story while modeling outstanding research strategy." In a starred review, *School Library Journal* called *Pathfinders: The Journeys of 16 Extraordinary Black Souls* a "masterly work." In a starred review of Bolden's Civil War–era novel *Crossing Ebenezer Creek, Kirkus Reviews* said this: "Informative, engrossing, and unflinching. . . . A poetic, raw, and extraordinary imagining of a little-known, shameful chapter in American history."
tonyaboldenbooks.com

Roy Boney Jr. is an award-winning Cherokee artist and writer whose work has been exhibited across the United States and internationally. He lives in Tahlequah, Oklahoma, and works for the Cherokee Nation in the tribe's language revitalization program. He obtained his BFA in design from Oklahoma State University and an MA in studio art from the University of Arkansas at Little Rock.
royboney.com

Vanessa Brantley-Newton celebrates self-love and acceptance of all cultures through her work, and hopes to inspire young readers to find their own voices. She first learned to express herself as a little girl through song. Growing up in a musical family, Vanessa's parents taught her how to sing to help overcome her stuttering. Each night the family would gather to make music together, with her mom on piano, her dad on guitar, and Vanessa and her sister, Coy, singing the blues, gospel, spirituals, and jazz. Now, whenever she illustrates, music fills the air and finds its way into her art. The children in her illustrations can be seen dancing, wiggling, and moving freely across the page in an expression of happiness. Music is a constant celebration, no matter the occasion, and Vanessa hopes her illustrations bring joy to others, with the magic of a beautiful melody.
vanessabrantleynewton.com

Tameka Fryer Brown is an award-winning picture book author. Her debut title, *Around Our Way on Neighbors' Day,* illustrated by Charlotte Riley-Webb, has sold more than 100,000 copies. Brown's second picture book, *My Cold Plum Lemon Pie Bluesy Mood,* illustrated by Shane W. Evans, received a Charlotte Zolotow Honor for excellence in picture book text and was designated a Bank Street College of Education Best Children's Book of the Year, a CCBC Choices Book, and one of New York Public Library's 100 Titles for Reading and Sharing.

Brown's third book, *Brown Baby Lullaby,* will be published in 2019. In the story, Momma and Papi struggle to get through the evening's routine with their strong-willed toddler—but they wouldn't have their sweet brown baby any other way.
tamekafryerbrown.com

Joseph Bruchac's commitment to social justice and cultural democracy includes marching with Dr. Martin Luther King Jr., three years of volunteer teaching in Ghana, eight years of running a college program inside a maximum-security prison, and decades of publishing multicultural work through his Greenfield Review Press.

He is the author of more than 130 books for readers of all ages, and his best-known books include the Keepers of the Earth series and *Code Talker*, a novel about the Navajo Marines who used their native language to create an unbreakable code in World War II. josephbruchac.com

Ashley Bryan was born in Harlem, New York, and grew up in the Bronx. He always had a love for writing and illustration and was educated at Cooper Union and Columbia University. Over the years, he taught painting and drawing in a number of schools and colleges, and he was a professor of art at Dartmouth College before leaving teaching to focus on his own work.

Ashley Bryan has published more than fifty books and has received numerous awards and recognitions, including multiple Coretta Scott King Awards, a Laura Ingalls Wilder Award, a *Boston Globe–Horn Book* Award, and a Newbery Honor. His books include *Freedom*

Over Me; Sail Away; Beautiful Blackbird; Beat the Story-Drum, Pum Pum; Let It Shine; Ashley Bryan's Puppets; and *What a Wonderful World*. He lives in Islesford, a small island off the coast of Maine, where at the age of ninety-four, he continues to paint, draw, and write. ashleybryancenter.org

Lesa Cline-Ransome's first book was the biography *Satchel Paige*, an ALA-ALSC Notable Children's Book and a Bank Street College Best Children's Book of the Year. She later created *Quilt Alphabet*, a collection of alphabet poems, and *Quilt Counting; Major Taylor: Champion Cyclist; Young Pelé: Soccer's First Star; Words Set Me Free; Light in the Darkness; Benny Goodman and Teddy Wilson; Freedom's School; My Story, My Dance; Just a Lucky So and So: The Story of Louis Armstrong;* and *Germs: Fact and Fiction, Friends and Foes.* Her newest title is the verse biography of Harriet Tubman, *Before She Was Harriet.* Lesa's books have received numerous honors and awards, including NAACP Image Awards, *Kirkus* Best Books of the Year recognition, two *Booklist* Top 10 Sports Books for Youth selections, and an Orbis Pictus Recommended Book. She lives in the Hudson Valley region of New York with her husband and frequent collaborator, James Ransome, and their family. lesaclineransome.com

Evelyn Coleman was the first African American to win the North Carolina Arts Council's $5,000 fiction fellowship. Her novel *Shadows on Society Hill* was American Girl doll Addy's first mystery and an Edgar Award nominee. *White Socks Only* was an ABA Best Pick of the List and a Smithsonian Notable Children's Book, and was selected by the Anti-Defamation League and Barnes & Noble's Close the Book on Hate campaign. *Freedom Train*, an NCSS-CBC Notable Social Studies Trade Book for Young People, is on the inaugural list of 25 Books All Young Georgians Should Read. *To Be a Drum*, a Skipping Stone Honor Book, is featured on Screen Actors Guild Book Pals, read by James Earl Jones.

Floyd Cooper began drawing at age three with pieces of plasterboard left by his father, who was working on the house. Now with more than one hundred children's books published, Floyd has established himself as a master craftsman of children's literature and illustration. He has received numerous awards, including Coretta Scott King Honors (*Brown Honey in Broomwheat Tea, Meet Danitra Brown, I Have Heard of a Land*), an NAACP Image Award (*Mandela*), a Jane Addams Children's Book Honor (*Ruth and the Green Book*), a Simon Wiesenthal Center/Museum of

Tolerance Once Upon a World Children's Book Award (*Ben and the Emancipation Proclamation*), an IPPY Gold Medal (*Ruth and the Green Book*), multiple ALA-ALSC Notables, Bank Street College of Education Best Children's Book Honors, Parents' Choice Honors, Junior Library Guild selections, and starred reviews from *Booklist, Kirkus Reviews,* and *School Library Journal.* He won the Coretta Scott King Award for *The Blacker the Berry,* and he is the artist for the 2018 U.S. Postal Service Kwanzaa Forever stamp. The Tulsa, Oklahoma, native makes his home in Easton, Pennsylvania, with his family wife Velma, sons Dayton and Kai, daughter-in-law Melissa, and grandson Niko.
floydcooper.com

Nina Crews has written and illustrated many energetic stories for young children, including *One Hot Summer Day, The Neighborhood Mother Goose,* and *Below.* She uses photographs and photo collages to create distinctive illustrations. Her work has been recognized by the ALA Notable Committee, the Cooperative Children's Book Council, the Junior Library Guild, and the Bank Street College of Education. Her latest book is *Seeing into Tomorrow: Haiku by Richard Wright.* She lives in Brooklyn, New York, with her husband and son.
ninacrews.com

Pat Cummings is the author and/or illustrator of more than thirty-five books. Pat also compiled and edited Talking with Artists, a series featuring notable children's book illustrators. Her Pratt and Parsons classes list a growing number of award-winning children's books creators. A frequent lecturer at schools, libraries, and conventions, she also conducts an annual Children's Book Boot Camp that connects writers and illustrators with agents and publishers.

Pat serves on the boards of the Authors Guild, the Authors League Fund, and SCBWI. She is a member of the Writers Guild of America East and is chair of the Society of Illustrators' Founders Award committee for the annual Original Art Show.

Her latest picture book, *Beauty and the Beast,* was translated and retold by her husband, H. Chuku Lee. Her debut middle-grade novel, *Trace,* is due in 2019.
patcummings.com

Nancy Devard is an engineer turned freelance artist/illustrator. After graduating from Temple University and working as a development engineer, she decided to pursue her passions—fine art and illustration. She worked as a staff artist for Hallmark Cards in Kansas City, Missouri, creating bestselling designs for the Mahogany and Kids

divisions. She is now a freelance children's book illustrator, working both traditionally and digitally. In 2008, she won a Coretta Scott King Illustration Honor Award for *The Secret Olivia Told Me,* published by Just Us Books, and she has illustrated other titles, including *From Where I Stand in the City* and *Puddin' Jeffrey and Leah: Best Friends.*

Sharon M. Draper is a professional educator, as well as an accomplished writer of more than thirty award-winning books for adolescents and teachers, including *Copper Sun,* winner of the Coretta Scott King Award; the highly acclaimed Jericho and Hazelwood trilogies; and *Out of My Mind,* the longtime *New York Times* bestseller. She served as the National Teacher of the Year during Bill Clinton's administration, has been honored at the White House six times, and was the U.S. State Department's literary ambassador to the children of Africa and China. In 2015, she was honored by the American Library Association as the recipient of the Margaret A. Edwards Award for lifetime literary achievement. Her newest novel is *Stella by Starlight.*
sharondraper.com

Zetta Elliott, born in Canada, moved to the United States in 1994 to pursue her PhD in American studies at NYU. Her poetry has been published in several anthologies, and her plays have been staged in New York and Chicago. Her essays have appeared in the *Huffington Post, School Library Journal,* and *Publishers Weekly.* She is the author of more than twenty-five books for young readers, including the award-winning picture book *Bird.* Her middle-grade fantasy novel *Ship of Souls* was named a *Booklist* Top 10 Sci-fi/Fantasy Title for Youth; her young adult novel *The Door at the Crossroads* was a finalist in the Speculative Fiction category of the Cybils Awards; and her picture book *Melena's Jubilee* won a Skipping Stone Award. Elliott is an advocate for greater diversity and equity in publishing. She currently lives in Brooklyn.
zettaelliott.com

Margarita Engle is the 2017–2019 national Young People's Poet Laureate, and the first Latino to receive that honor. She is the Cuban American author of many verse novels, including *The Surrender Tree,* a Newbery Honor winner, and *The Lightning Dreamer,* a PEN USA Award winner. Her verse memoir, *Enchanted Air,* received the Pura Belpré Award, the Golden Kite Award, a Walter Dean Myers Honor, the Lee Bennett Hopkins Poetry Award, and the Arnold Adoff Poetry Award, among others. *Drum Dream Girl* received the Charlotte Zolotow Award for best picture book text. Her newest verse novel about the island is *Forest World,* and her newest picture books are *All the Way to Havana* and *Miguel's Brave Knight: Young Cervantes and His Dream of Don Quixote.* Forthcoming books include *The Flying Girl: How Aída de Acosta Learned to Soar* and *Jazz Owls: A Novel of the Zoot Suit Riots.* Margarita was born in Los Angeles but developed a deep attachment to her mother's homeland during childhood summers with relatives. She was trained as an agronomist and botanist. She lives in central California with her husband.
margaritaengle.com |
@YPPLaureate

Zamani Feelings is a portrait, event, and sports photographer located in Philadelphia. The love for photography was born from his initial interest in documentary film. Zamani was drawn to photography in an attempt to capture the same feeling, emotion, and story of cinematic film and translate those dynamics into still imagery. His experience is vast and spans from portrait and wedding photography to newspaper and web photojournalism, as well as his latest passion for sports photography. Zamani currently photographs college football and basketball for Temple University athletics and NFL football for Vavel USA, and is the official sports photographer for the William Penn Charter School. He also teaches sports photography workshops at the Philadelphia Photo Arts Center.
zamanifeelings.com |
zamanifeelings.net

Sharon G. Flake, with millions of books in print, is considered to be one of the top authors in young adult literature. The winner of multiple Coretta Scott King Awards, she has penned nine novels and one picture book—*You Are Not a Cat!* Her breakout novel, *The Skin I'm In,* established her as a favorite among middle school and high school students, and a go-to author for teachers and librarians eager to get their students excited about reading.

With its universal themes, Sharon's work is read around the globe. She has been published in multiple languages, including Korean, French, and Portuguese. Her books top many prestigious lists, including *Kirkus Reviews* Best Teen Books of the Year, Chicago Public Library Best of the Best Books, *Booklist* Top 10 Books for Youth, New York Public Library Books for the Teen Age, Detroit Library Books of the Year, Top 100 Books for Teenage Girls, Texas Lone Star Reading List, Bank Street College of Education Best Children's Books of the Year, and others.

sharongflake.com

Bernette G. Ford

was born in Brooklyn and grew up in Uniondale, Long Island, New York. She worked for more than forty years in children's book publishing, where she published many bestselling books. In 2002, she left corporate publishing to start her own children's book packaging company, Color-Bridge Books. Semi-retired since 2014, she now has more time to write, and to freelance with UK children's book company Boxer Books as their American editor.

Bernette has collaborated with her husband, George, on only a few titles—one of their favorites being *Bright Eyes, Brown Skin,* which Bernette co-authored with Cheryl Willis Hudson. The couple have one grown daughter who lives and works in New Orleans as an editor, writer, and consultant on HIV, health, gender, and justice.

George Ford has

illustrated countless books for children, one of the most popular being *The Story of Ruby Bridges.* He has worked as a graphic designer and early on as a greeting-card artist. He was raised in Bedford Stuyvesant, Brooklyn, but lived as a young child on the island of Barbados with his sister and maternal grandmother. He studied at Cooper Union, the Pratt Institute, and the School of Visual Arts, and earned a Bachelors in Art Education from City College, although he never taught. He has been married to Bernette Ford since 1978, and has found his most satisfying projects working with Wade and Cheryl Hudson, founders of Just Us Books, the children's book press begun in 1988.

Laura Freeman,

originally from New York City, now lives in Atlanta with her husband and their two children. She received her BFA from the School of Visual Arts and began her career working for various editorial clients. She has illustrated more than twenty children's books, including *Hidden Figures: The True Story of Four Black Women and the Space Race,* written by Margot Lee Shetterly; *Fancy Party Gowns* by Deborah Blumenthal; and the Nikki & Deja series by Karen English.

In addition to illustrating books and editorial content, Laura's art can be found on a wide range of products, from dishes and textiles to greeting cards.

lfreemanart.com

Chester Higgins Jr.'s photographs

have been published widely in the *New York Times,* from which he retired as a staff photographer in 2015. He has exhibited in museums around the world. His most recent exhibition opened in October 2017 at the Virginia Museum of Fine Arts. He has produced seven books; most recently his photographs illustrate *Ancient Nubia: African Kingdoms on the Nile.* He is the author of *Feeling the Spirit: Searching the World for the People of Africa, Elder Grace: The Nobility of Aging,* and *Echo of the Spirit: A Photographer's Journey.*

chesterhiggins.com

Ekua Holmes is a native of Roxbury, Massachusetts, and a graduate of the Massachusetts College of Art and Design. Her first children's book, *Voice of Freedom: Fannie Lou Hamer, Spirit of the Civil Rights Movement*, won a Caldecott Honor, a Robert F. Sibert Honor, and a *Boston Globe–Horn Book* Honor. She also illustrated Newbery Award winner Kwame Alexander's book *Out of Wonder: Poems Celebrating Poets*.

She uses mixed media collage and layers newspaper, photos, fabric, and other materials to create colorful compositions. As a young artist, Holmes discovered the power of found objects, which derive their identity as art from places as well as the social histories attached to the objects. Many of Ekua's collages are reminiscent of the late Romare Bearden and Njideka Akunyili. About her work, Holmes says, "In everything I create I hear them saying, 'Remember me,' and through my work I honor their legacies by bringing them forward to life.... With these scraps and remnants, assembled like a down-home quilt, I rebuild my world, putting in what speaks to my personal and cultural narrative." ekuaholmes.com

Cheryl Willis Hudson is an author, editor, and cofounder–editorial director of Just Us Books, an independent company that focuses on Black-interest books for children and young adults. Cheryl has written more than two dozen books for young children, including *Bright Eyes, Brown Skin* (with Bernette G. Ford); *Afro-Bets ABC Book; Good Morning, Baby; Glo Goes Shopping; From Where I Stand in the City; Clothes I Love to Wear; Hands Can; Construction Zone;* and *My Friend Maya Loves to Dance*. She has also coedited a number of titles, including *How Sweet the Sound: African American Songs for Children*.

Cheryl is a member of the children's book committee of PEN America and has served as a diversity consultant to a number of educational publishers. Outside of her full-time immersion in children's books, Cheryl enjoys a cappella singing and creating handmade story quilts.
cherylwhudson.weebly.com

Curtis Hudson is a musician/ songwriter/ producer who has been playing and composing music since the age of twelve. He began his musical career playing in church and for gospel and R&B groups in Louisiana. During his early twenties, he composed music for three regional plays written by his brother Wade Hudson. As a member of the group Pure Energy, Curtis composed and produced most of the group's music. He composed the hit song "Holiday" sung by Madonna (cowritten by Lisa Stevens), the hit song "Body Work" for the movie *Breakin',* and the mega hit "Lose Control" by Missy Elliott. Curtis is also the father of the multiplatinum music producer Eric Hudson.

Stephan J. Hudson is a graphic artist and photographer. A graduate of Rowan University in New Jersey, where he received a bachelor's degree in graphic arts, Stephan operates his own photography studio, 2ndchapterphoto, located in East Orange, New Jersey. Stephan is also a book designer, and his photos and artwork have illustrated such picture books as *Poetry from the Masters: The Pioneers* and *Prayers for the Smallest Hands*. Stephan says, "In today's world of iPhones, smart devices, and digital cameras, anyone has the ability to take a great photo at least once. However, it is the artist known as a photographer who has the ability to create and re-create great imagery."
2ndchapterphoto.com

Wade Hudson is president and CEO of Just Us Books, an independent publisher of Black-interest books for children and young adults. Among his thirty published titles are *Book of Black Heroes from A to Z, Jamal's Busy Day, Pass It On: African American Poetry for Children, Powerful Words: More Than 200 Years of Extraordinary Writing by African Americans, It's Church*

Going Time, and *Feelings I Love to Share* and *Friends I Love to Keep.* He has received a New Jersey Stephen Crane Literary Award; the Ida B. Wells Institutional Leadership Award, presented by the Center for Black Literature; and the Madame C. J. Walker Legacy Award, given by the Hurston/Wright Foundation. He has also been inducted into the International Literary Hall of Fame for Writers of African Descent. wadehudson-authorpublisher.com

Hena Khan is a picture book and middle grade author. Her recent middle grade novel is *Amina's Voice,* the first release of Simon & Schuster's Salaam Reads. She is the author of the *Zayd Saleem: Chasing the Dream* chapter book series, in addition to several picture books including *Golden Domes and Silver Lanterns* and *It's Ramadan, Curious George.* Hena is a native of Maryland, where she still lives with her family. henakhan.com

Rafael López is an internationally recognized illustrator and artist. Growing up in Mexico City, he was immersed in the rich cultural heritage and native color of street life. Influenced by Mexican surrealism and myths, he developed a style with roots in these traditions. He has won

Pura Belpré Medals for his illustrations for *Drum Dream Girl* and *Book Fiesta!* He won the Tomás Rivera Children's Book Award for a book about his community mural work, and he was awarded the Society of Illustrators Original Art Silver Medal. In 2012, López was selected by the Library of Congress to create the National Book Festival poster, and his work has earned multiple Pura Belpré Honors and Américas Awards. The illustrations created by López bring diverse characters to children's books, and he is driven to produce and promote books that reflect and honor the lives of all young people. rafaellopez.com

Kelly Starling Lyons is a children's book author and founding member of The Brown Bookshelf (thebrownbookshelf.com), a team of authors and illustrators dedicated to raising awareness of black children's book creators. As a kid, she rarely saw stories for young readers that featured characters of color. Her mission is to make sure children today have a different reality. Her books include *NEATE: Eddie's Ordeal;* CCBC Choices picture book *One Million Men and Me; Ellen's Broom,* a Coretta Scott King Illustrator Honor Book and a Junior Library Guild and Bank Street Best Children's Book selection; *Tea Cakes for Tosh* and *Hope's Gift,* both NCSS-CBC Notable Social Studies Trade Books for Young

People; and *One More Dino on the Floor,* a Scholastic Reading Club pick. Her new chapter book series debuted in September with two titles: *Jada Jones: Rock Star* and *Jada Jones: Class Act.* kellystarlinglyons.com

Tony Medina is the author of six beloved books for young readers, including *The President Looks Like Me & Other Poems; I and I, Bob Marley;* and *Love to Langston,* as well as multiple volumes of poetry. A Pushcart Prize–nominated poet and professor of creative writing at Howard University, Dr. Medina is a two-time winner of the Paterson Prize for Books for Young People. His most recent books are the graphic novel *I Am Alfonso Jones* and *Thirteen Ways of Looking at a Black Boy.* tonymedina.org/books.html

Mansa K. Mussa is a visual artist, arts educator, and arts consultant and exhibit curator. A native of Paterson, New Jersey, he has used the camera to document the unfolding of human events in the United States, the Caribbean, Africa, Central America, and Europe for the past forty years. He earned a BA in media arts and television production from New Jersey City University and studied visual art there with Professor Emeritus Ben Jones. Mussa has been an instructor of photography and visual arts for thirty-eight years. During that time, he has developed a system for teaching art to children, teens, adults, sensational seniors, and the special needs population. He currently teaches photography, collage, wearable art, book arts, mask making, and iPadology for Arts Horizons, the Newark Museum, AileyCamp/Newark, the Visual Arts Center of New Jersey, the New Jersey Performing Arts Center, Global Arts to Go, and Arts Unbound. artistsofthevalley.org/mansakmussa

Innosanto Nagara is a children's author, activist, and graphic designer. He is the author of the bestselling alphabet book *A Is for Activist*, as well as *Counting on Community*, *My Night in the Planetarium*, and *The Wedding Portrait*. According to an interview on NPR, Nagara began writing children's books upon realizing that he could not find "a fun book" that "talked about the importance of social justice." Nagara was born and raised in Jakarta, Indonesia, and moved to the United States in 1988. He studied zoology and philosophy at UC Davis, then moved to the San Francisco Bay Area, where he worked as a graphic designer for a range of social change organizations, before founding the Design Action Collective, a worker-owned cooperative design studio in Oakland, California. aisforactivist.com

Marilyn Nelson is the author or translator of twenty-four poetry books, among them *The Fields of Praise: New and Selected Poems; Carver: A Life in Poems; Fortune's Bones;* and *A Wreath for Emmett Till.* Other award-winning books are the recently published *How I Discovered Poetry* and *My Seneca Village.* Nelson's honors include two NEA creative writing fellowships, the Connecticut Arts Award, a Fulbright teaching fellowship, a fellowship from the John Simon Guggenheim Memorial Foundation, the Frost Medal, the NSK Neustadt Prize for Children's Literature, and the NCTE Award for Excellence in Poetry for Children. She was the poet laureate of the state of Connecticut from 2001 to 2006. marilyn-nelson.com

Ellen Oh is cofounder, president, and CEO of We Need Diverse Books (WNDB), a nonprofit organization dedicated to increasing diversity in children's literature. A former adjunct college instructor and corporate attorney, she is the author of the middle-grade novel *The Spirit Hunters*, Book 1 and the YA fantasy trilogy the Prophecy series. She is also the editor of WNDB's middle-grade anthology *Flying Lessons and Other Stories* and the upcoming YA anthology *A Thousand Beginnings and Endings.* Originally from New York City, Ellen lives in Bethesda, Maryland, with her husband and three children and has yet to satisfy her quest for a decent bagel. ellenoh.com

Denise Lewis Patrick, a Louisiana native transplanted to New Jersey, has written everything from poetry to puzzles to plays. She has written more than two dozen books for children and young adults, such as the picture books *Red Dancing Shoes* and *Ma Dear's Old Green House.* Her middle-grade novels

include *The Adventures of Midnight Son, Finding Someplace,* and *No Ordinary Sound.* She is also an amateur artist and doll maker, as well as an adjunct writing professor. Her words here and her heart go out to every young reader, especially her new granddaughter, Olympia!
deniselewispatrick.com

Andrea Pippins is an illustrator, designer, and author who has a passion for creating images that reflect what she wants to see in art, media, and pop culture. Her vision is to empower people of color with tools and inspiration to create and tell their own stories. Andrea is the creator of the bestselling coloring book *I Love My Hair* and the interactive journal *Becoming Me.* Her clients include *Scoop* Magazine, *Family Circle,* the *Huffington Post, Bustle,* Free People, Lincoln Center, and the National Museum of African American History and Culture. Andrea is based in Stockholm. Her newest title is *Young, Gifted, and Black,* written by Jamia Wilson.
andreapippins.com | @andreapippins

James E. Ransome is an illustrator and painter, with works exhibited in both private and public art collections. A graduate of the Pratt Institute, James has illustrated more than sixty books for children. He has received the *Boston Globe–Horn Book* Honor and the Pratt Institute Alumni Achievement Award, as well as recognition by the Society of Illustrators. Other awards include the Coretta Scott King Honor Award, an IBBY award, two NAACP Image Awards, the Simon Wiesenthal Center/Museum of Tolerance Once Upon a World Children's Book Award, the Rip Van Winkle Award, a SEBA Book Award, and the Dutchess County Executive's Arts Award for Individual Artist. A number of his books have received ALA-ALSC Notable Children's Book distinctions.

James is also an associate professor in the School of Art at Syracuse University. He has a traveling exhibit entitled *Everyday People: The Art of James E. Ransome,* hosted with the National Center for Children's Illustrated Literature (NCCIL) museum in Abilene, Texas. James lives in the Hudson Valley region of New York with his wife and frequent collaborator, children's books author Lesa Cline-Ransome.
jamesransome.com

Jason Reynolds is crazy. About stories. He is a *New York Times* bestselling author, a two-time National Book Award honoree, a *Kirkus* Prize winner, a Walter Dean Myers Award winner, an NAACP Image Award winner, and the recipient of multiple Coretta Scott King Honors. His debut novel, *When I Was the Greatest,* was followed by the YA novel *The Boy in the Black Suit* and *All American Boys* (cowritten with Brendan Kiely), both of which won Coretta Scott King Honors, as well as the critically acclaimed middle-grade novel *As Brave as You,* the first three books in the Track series, *Ghost, Patina,* and *Sunny,* and the YA novels *Miles Morales: Spider Man* and *Long Way Down.*
jasonwritesbooks.com

Olugbemisola Rhuday-Perkovich is the author of *8th Grade Superzero,* which was named an ILA Notable Book for a Global Society and an NCSS-CBC Notable Social Studies Trade Book for Young People. She is the coauthor of the middle-grade novels *Two Naomis,* which was nominated for an NAACP Image Award, and *Naomis Too.* Olugbemisola has contributed to several anthologies, including *Open Mic: Riffs on Life Between Cultures in Ten Voices, Imagine It Better: Visions of What School Might Be,* and *The Journey Is Everything: Teaching Essays That Students Want to Write for People Who Want to Read Them.* She is a member of The Brown Bookshelf and We Need Diverse Books. Olugbemisola holds an MA in education and writes frequently on education and parenting topics. She lives with her family in New York City, where she writes, makes things, and needs to get more sleep.
olugbemisolabooks.com

Edel Rodriguez was born in 1971 in Havana, Cuba. His family immigrated to the United States in 1980 on the Mariel boatlift and settled in Miami. He graduated from the Pratt Institute in Brooklyn in 1994 with a degree in painting and graphic design, then worked briefly at *Spy* magazine. After joining *Time* magazine as a designer, for ten years he served as the art director of *Time*'s Canadian and Latin American editions. As a freelance illustrator, he has worked for MTV, the *New Yorker*, the *New York Times*, *New York Magazine*, the *Nation*, the *Village Voice*, *Rolling Stone*, and *Time*. His award-winning illustrations have appeared in *American Illustration* and *Communication Arts*. Edel's picture books include *Mama Does the Mambo* by Katherine Leiner, *Float Like a Butterfly* by Ntozake Shange, *Sonia Sotomayor: A Judge Grows in the Bronx / La juez que creció en el Bronx* by Jonah Winter, and *Oye, Celia!* by Katie Sciurba. *Sergio Makes a Splash!* is his debut book as author and illustrator.
edelrodriguez.com

Charles R. Smith Jr. is an award-winning author, photographer, and poet with more than thirty books to his credit. His awards include a Coretta Scott King Award for Illustration for his photographs accompanying the Langston Hughes poem *My People* and a Coretta Scott King Author Honor for his biography of Muhammad Ali, *Twelve Rounds to Glory.* Charles speaks to kids in schools all over the country about the importance of connecting the mind, body, and spirit to accomplish any goal. He recently achieved a major accomplishment when he was chosen to compete on season nine of *American Ninja Warrior.* Unfortunately, he didn't finish the course, but he did get to the middle and had a great time doing it.
charlesrsmithjr.com

Javaka Steptoe is a *New York Times* bestselling author/illustrator, eclectic artist, designer, and illustrator who has built a national reputation as an outstanding contributor to children's literature. His debut work, *In Daddy's Arms I Am Tall: African Americans Celebrating Fathers,* earned him the Coretta Scott King Illustrator Award and an NAACP Image Award nomination. He was awarded the Caldecott Medal for *Radiant Child: The Story of Young Artist Jean-Michel Basquiat.* Utilizing everyday objects, from aluminum plates to pocket lint, and sometimes illustrating with a jigsaw and paint, he delivers reflective and thoughtful collage creations filled with vitality, playful energy, and strength. Steptoe earned his Bachelor of Fine Arts degree from Cooper Union. Committed to children's education, he makes appearances at schools, libraries, museums, and conferences across the country. His other illustrated books include *Do You Know What I'll Do?, A Pocketful of Poems, Hot Day on Abbott Avenue, The Jones Family Express, Rain Play,* and *Jimi: Sounds Like a Rainbow.*
javaka.com

Eleanora E. Tate is the author of eleven novels and numerous short stories for middle-grade readers. Her award-winning books include *Just an Overnight Guest,* adapted into a television film; *The Secret of Gumbo Grove; Thank You, Dr. Martin Luther King, Jr.!; A Blessing in Disguise; Front Porch Stories at the One-Room School;* and *Celeste's Harlem Renaissance* (an IRA Teachers' Choice). A Drake University graduate and a longtime journalist, she was an instructor with the Institute of Children's Literature and taught children's literature at North Carolina Central University and in Hamline University's Writing for Children and Young Adults MFA program. The South Carolina State House and Senate cited her for her literary and community activism in 1990. She's also a Zora Neale Hurston Award recipient, the highest award given by the National Association of Black Storytellers, and is a former national president of the organization.
eleanoraetate.com

Eric Velasquez was born in Spanish Harlem and grew up in Harlem. He earned his BFA from the School of Visual Arts and has been illustrating for more than thirty years, including numerous book jackets and interior illustrations. Eric's first picture book, *The Piano Man* by Debbi Chocolate, won the Coretta Scott King–John Steptoe Award for New Talent. Eric was awarded an NAACP Image Award for his work in *Our Children Can Soar*, which he collaborated on with twelve notable illustrators of children's literature. Eric also wrote and illustrated *Grandma's Records* and its follow-up, *Grandma's Gift*, which won the Pura Belpré Award for illustration and was nominated for an NAACP Image Award. Eric's latest book, *Schomburg: The Man Who Built a Library* by Carole Boston Weatherford, has earned rave reviews. Eric Velasquez lives and works in New York, and he teaches book illustration at the Fashion Institute of Technology.
ericvelasquez.com

Carole Boston Weatherford is a *New York Times* bestselling author of dozens of books, including *Freedom in Congo Square*, winner of Caldecott and Coretta Scott King Honors; *Gordon Parks: How the Photographer Captured Black and White America*, winner of an NAACP Image Award; *Voice of Freedom: Fannie Lou Hamer, Spirit of the Civil Rights Movement*, winner of a Caldecott Honor; *Moses: When Harriet Tubman Led Her People to Freedom*, winner of an NAACP Image Award, a Caldecott Honor, and a Coretta Scott King Award for Illustration; and *Becoming Billie Holiday*, winner of a Coretta Scott King Author Honor. The recipient of the North Carolina Award for Literature, Carole teaches at Fayetteville State University.
cbweatherford.com

Jeffery B. Weatherford is an award-winning children's book illustrator and spoken word poet. *You Can Fly: The Tuskegee Airmen* was named an ALA-ALSC Notable Children's Book, an NCSS-CBC Notable Social Studies Trade book selection, and a best book of the year by the National Council for the Social Studies, the Cooperative Children's Book Center, the New York Public Library, and *Kirkus Reviews*. Through Great Brain Entertainment, he produces content for many media platforms. His fine art has been shown in Washington, Baltimore, Atlanta, and around North Carolina. Jeffery holds an MFA in painting from Howard University.
jbweatherford.wordpress.com

Rita Williams-Garcia is the celebrated author of a dozen acclaimed books for children and teens. Her best-known title, *One Crazy Summer*, received the Coretta Scott King Author Award, the Newbery Honor, the Scott O'Dell Award for Historical Fiction, the Parents' Choice Award, and the Junior Library Guild Award. *Clayton Byrd Goes Underground*, *One Crazy Summer* and *Jumped* were named National Book Award finalists, while *P.S. Be Eleven* also received the Coretta Scott King Author Award. Her other notable titles, including *Every Time a Rainbow Dies*, *Catching the Wild Waiyuuzee*, *No Laughter Here*, *Like Sisters on the Homefront*, *Fast Talk on a Slow Track*, *Blue Tights*, and *Gone Crazy in Alabama*, have received numerous citations. *Bottle Cap Boys Dancing on Royal Street* is her second picture book. Rita served on the faculty of the Vermont College of Fine Arts MFA program for writing for children and young adults. She resides in Queens, New York, with her husband and has two adult daughters. When Rita isn't writing, she is knitting, daydreaming, and boxing.
rita-williamsgarcia
.squarespace.com

Jacqueline Woodson is the sixth National Ambassador for Young People's Literature, 2018–2019, and the 2014 National Book Award winner for her memoir *Brown Girl Dreaming*, which received the Coretta Scott King Award, a Newbery Honor, the NAACP Image Award, and the Sibert Honor. She is also the author of the award-winning novel *Another Brooklyn*, which was a National Book Award finalist and Woodson's first adult novel in twenty years. In 2015, Woodson was named the Young People's Poet Laureate by the Poetry Foundation. She is the author of more than two dozen award-winning books for young adults, middle graders, and children; among her many accolades, she is a four-time Newbery Honor winner, a three-time National Book Award finalist, and a two-time Coretta Scott King Award winner.

jacquelinewoodson.com

Photography Credits

p. 17: Ellen and Janet Ha, photograph by Don Ha, Ellen Oh private collection
p. 22: Cheryl Willis Hudson private collection
p. 27: Bernette G. Ford private collection
p. 74: Jabari Asim photograph by Shef Reynolds II
p. 75: Vanessa Brantley-Newton photograph by Syreena Homer
p. 76: Joseph Bruchac photograph by Eric Jenks; Lesa Cline-Ransome photograph by Dawn Sela
p. 77: Pat Cummings photograph by Marvin Lee
p. 78: Margarita Engle photograph by Marshall W. Johnson; Sharon G. Flake photograph by Sandidge Photography
p. 80: Cheryl Willis Hudson, Curtis Hudson, and Wade Hudson photographs by 2ndchapterphoto
p. 81: Tony Medina photograph by Aldon Lynn Nielsen
p. 82: Ellen Oh photograph by Robin Shotola
p. 84: Edel Rodriguez photograph by Glen Glasser, Eleanora E. Tate photograph by Zack E. Hamlett III

Index